To Uncle Remus, Aunt Jemima, and all the singers/storytellers of yore, but most
especially my grandfather John Brown Watson — N. G.

To Vladimir — C. R.

Library of Congress Cataloging-in-Publication Data is available. Library of Congress Catalog Card Number 2006051849.
ISBN 978-0-7636-3021-8. Printed in Singapore. This book was typeset in Cygnet. The illustrations were done in watercolor.
Candlewick Press, 2067 Massachusetts Avenue, Cambridge, Massachusetts 02140. Visit us at www.candlewick.com.
10 9 8 7 6 5 4 3 2 1

THE GRASSHOPPER'S SONG
∽∾ AN AESOP'S FABLE REVISITED ∽∾

NIKKI GIOVANNI   CHRIS RASCHKA

CANDLEWICK PRESS
CAMBRIDGE, MASSACHUSETTS

THE CAST OF CHARACTERS

THE PLAINTIFF
James "Jimmy"
Ignatius Grasshopper

COUNSELS FOR THE PLAINTIFF
Robin, Robin, Robin, and Wren

Judge
Oscar Owl

Court Bailiff

Witnesses for the Plaintiff

THE DEFENDANTS
Nestor and Abigail
Ant

COUNSELS FOR THE DEFENSE
Moth, Moth, Butterfly, and Slug

THE JURY

Jimmy Grasshopper was furious. "All summer long, I sang for them. All summer I gave them the beat by which they harvested their food. Even in the evening, when we all were tired, I played a melody to keep up our spirits. I never thought they would turn their backs on me. It's just not right."

Henry Sr. adjusted his glasses. "Did they ask you to sing?"

"Well . . . no. But they enjoyed my music."

"I'm not sure how we should proceed, Jimmy. You provided a service they didn't request."

"That's true. But they used it. They accepted my offer by letting me work alongside them every day. Will you take my case? Will you sue the Ants for me?"

"And what will we sue them for?" asked Henry Sr.

"Respect," said Jimmy Grasshopper. "R-E-S-P-E-C-T."

The next day, Henry Sr. called a meeting of the partners,
Robin, Robin, Robin, and Wren.

"Jimmy Grasshopper feels he is not respected by the Ants for the work he has done. He wants us to sue. What do you think?"

The first one to speak was Lori Wren. "Jimmy is right. Almost every year, one of the Grasshoppers comes to make music. I have my office windows open and hear the most wonderful sounds. He should be paid."

Henry Jr. spoke next. "It will be a tricky case, because the Ants didn't actually contract with the Grasshoppers for a service."

Uncle Leo Robin spoke last. "When we started this firm"—he looked at Henry Jr.—"your father and I, we wanted to stand up for what is right. We have done well. We sued the Beavers and won when they wanted that dam upstream that would have changed our water table.

"We sued the Woodpeckers when they were trying to take that silver maple down before its time. Even when Old Badger wanted to move into the Rabbits' warren and everyone thought we would lose because the Badgers had threatened so many of the jurors, we didn't take low. We stood up. We stood for those who needed the protection of the law.

"It seems to me, whether we win or not, that Jimmy Grasshopper and his family have given enough to the Ants. Every year the same thing happens. The Grasshoppers sing, the Ants work in rhythm, the crops come up smoothly, and when winter comes, the Ants turn their backs. It's time to take a stand. What say you?"

Robin, Robin, and Wren said, "Yes."

Motions were filed and depositions taken.
All through a snowy, icy winter,
the underground buzz
was about the case.

At the first sign of spring, Judge Oscar Owl called a
jury. He didn't want to lose the residents who would need
to head for their summer homes.

The courtroom was packed.

"Well, I think it was very brave of Jimmy Grasshopper to bring this action," said Sammy Gnat.

"Foolish," replied Terry Termite. "I heard him sing and play all last summer, and I don't owe him a thing. I hope I get on that jury."

He didn't, but his cousin Timothy did.

The members of the jury were

Tilly
Titmouse

Barry Beaver

Patricia
Sparrow

William H.
Weasel III

Timothy Termite

Minnie Mole

Sydney Fox

Evelyn
Yellow-Finch

Christopher
Rabbit

J. Thomas Turtle Jr.

Jenny Gnat

The alternates were
Billy Flea and Michael Mosquito

Lisa Cricket

Opening statements were due
the very next day.

"All rise," cried the bailiff. "Hear ye, hear ye, hear ye.
The Honorable Judge Oscar Owl."

"Please be seated," said the judge. "The court is ready to hear the matter of James Ignatius Grasshopper versus Nestor and Abigail Ant. Is counsel ready for opening statements?"

Henry Jr. rose to his feet. "The plaintiff is ready, Your Honor."

Osceola Slug of Moth, Moth, Butterfly, and Slug rolled to her feet.

"The defense is ready, Judge Owl."

Young Henry walked over to the jury. "What is the worth of art?" he began. "That is the question this case poses." Young Henry took a deep breath and continued:

"Jimmy Grasshopper and his family have sung for years, helping the Ants by providing the rhythm to which they smoothly harvest their crops. All summer, when it is warm and food and water are plentiful, the Ants welcome the Grasshoppers into their camps. The Grasshoppers make beautiful music. And that is without dispute.

"You will, throughout this trial, hear expert testimony about the benefits of music. It has been proven that those who sing, those who make music, play a key role in the survival of all life — mammals, reptiles, amphibians, birds, fish, and insects.

"Parents sing their babies to sleep. Sleeping babies are less likely to attract predators. When the young hear music, even in the larval stage, even in the womb, they respond to soothing sounds. They are calmer and therefore learn the ways of the community more easily. Generation after generation of Ants—who are without a soothing voice—have benefited from this generous gift of the Grasshoppers." He paused, flapped his wings as if in supplication, and looked perplexed.

"My client, Jimmy Grasshopper, is seeking reasonable reparations of respect. But since respect cannot be quantified, the firm of Robin, Robin, Robin, and Wren is seeking fifty percent of the summer bounty as just and lawful compensation. When you have heard all the testimony, I am sure you will all agree. Thank you."

Osceola Slug rose to her full height. She sauntered to the jury.

"This case, I am sure you will see, is a simple case of who worked and who didn't. All summer, Mr. Grasshopper wrote songs and did funny dances. Of course my clients enjoyed it. Who doesn't enjoy a clown? But my clients repeatedly asked Mr. Grasshopper, 'Shouldn't you be storing food for the winter? Shouldn't you be in the process of preparation for the cold months?' Each time, *each* time, Mr. Grasshopper assured my clients that he was content with his merrymaking. 'Winter will take care of itself,' he said. Now he finds himself with nothing. Is this the responsibility of Nestor and Abigail Ant? Mr. Grasshopper chose not to prepare for the future. Well, ladies and gentlemen of the jury, we are asking you to send a message. Those who fritter summer away will have to pay winter's price."

She twirled around and sat.

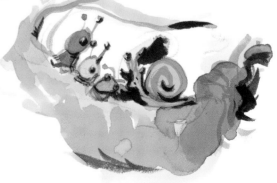

The counsel for the plaintiff called James Ignatius Grasshopper to the stand. He sat straight and tall in the witness chair. He told of his father's service, his aunts' and uncles' service, the service through the years that his family had offered the Ants.

"Why," asked Lori Wren on direct, "do you think you are owed respect when you did not work to earn it? What makes you think you should be granted one-half of the bounty Nestor and Abigail Ant and their family earned?"

Jimmy sat even taller.

"Am I not worthy of my bread? Does not the work of my heart and soul earn respect? I am an artist. Is there no place for beauty, no solace for the ear, no hope for the heart? Must everything be in the marketplace? Doesn't the marketplace itself need and deserve beautification?

"Artists tell the stories that entertain and instruct; we tell the jokes that make you laugh, thereby keeping you happy and healthy; we describe the beauty of nature in ways that can make you weep with awe at the marvels of a Higher Power. Without art, life would be a big mistake. It is art that speaks to a higher good in us; it is art that reminds us our immortal souls should seek a higher purpose; it is art that gives us not only the words for love but also the reason for it."

Lori Wren looked in the direction of the defendants. "Your witness," she said.

Amy Moth fluttered to the front.

"Mr. Grasshopper, did my clients ask you to sing? Did they ask any of your relatives to sing? At any time was there any indication of a contract? Were you hired for services rendered?"

"Objection, Your Honor," exclaimed Henry Robin Sr. "Counsel is badgering the witness!"

"Overruled," said Judge Owl. "The witness may answer the questions."

"Yes or no, Mr. Grasshopper? Did they promise you anything?"

"No," said Jimmy.

"Did my clients ever ask you to come and perform for them?"

"You don't understand. I—"

"Yes or no, Mr. Grasshopper?"

"Well, no, but that's not the whole story."

With a satisfied smile, Amy Moth fluttered. "No more questions," she said, and wriggled back to her seat.

Judge Owl said, "The witness may step down."

"But, Your Honor, she didn't give me a chance to fully answer."

The judge looked down at Jimmy. "Step down, Mr. Grasshopper," he said without a smile.

The plaintiff next called Dr. Michael Secretary-Bird, a renowned anthropologist from Kenya, who testified about the necessity of art to development. His testimony examined how the art community ultimately gave rise to cities as we know them—not, as many had thought, the other way around. The guild workers' desire to be close to each other, to share ideas as much as to trade goods, resulted in the place we now call the city.

Julia Moth walked slowly to the witness chair.

"Dr. Secretary-Bird, in all you have explained to us this afternoon, am I correct in thinking that you have, in essence, given us the reasons why cities were created?"

"Yes, that's correct."

"You have described the various needs of creatures to come together for mutual protection, both physical and emotional. Is that correct?"

"Yes, it is."

"When these workers interacted, would you say they were trading?"

"Yes, I would."

"Would it be fair to say that each party was honoring a contract? An agreement to accept goods for services rendered and vice versa?"

"I suppose that is fair to say."

"Well, what happens when there is no contract? When no one asks for the service provided? How can we assess work when no work was done?"

Lori Wren was on her feet. "Objection, Your Honor! It has not been established that no work has been done!" she exclaimed. "Ms. Moth knows very well that 'work' has not been defined."

"Sustained," said the judge.

"Indeed," Lori asked on redirect, "what is a contract? A piece of paper signed by two parties, or an agreement, spoken or unspoken?"

She paused. No one spoke.

"Dr. Secretary-Bird," she continued, "in all your studies, in all your travels, in all your vast wisdom, where, in your considered opinion, would we be if we did not honor our contracts? If we did not keep our word?"

"I think we would be lawless."

"No further questions," she said. "The plaintiff rests, Your Honor."

Judge Owl looked at the defendants' table. "Call your first witness."

"The defense calls Nestor Ant."

Nestor told how the Grasshoppers and the Ants were together in the summer, but when winter came, the Grasshoppers always went one way and the Ants another. He was surprised, he said, when there was a knock at his door last year. It was one of the coldest days of winter, and he couldn't imagine who would be out in this weather. It was Jimmy Grasshopper. He wanted to come into their home and sleep until the weather changed.

"Did you invite him in?" asked Myra Butterfly. "Did you greet him as a friend? Did you express any concern for why he was there?"

"Indeed not. I told him in no uncertain terms that he must leave my door."

"And then what happened, sir?"

"Why, he called me the most vile names. He shouted so loudly, my children could hear."

"Then what did you do?"

"Do? I had Abigail call the police to remove him. I feared for the safety of my family."

Myra Butterfly turned to Robin, Robin, Robin, and Wren. "Your witness."

39

Uncle Leo Robin approached the witness stand. "Do you value beauty?" he asked.

Nestor Ant answered. "Yes, I do. But just because we enjoyed his music doesn't mean we owe him half our work. We urged him to work and save."

We warned him that bad days were coming. But Jimmy just kept on playing."

"No further questions, Your Honor," said Uncle Leo.

The defense called Abigail Ant to the stand.

"Did you think you *owed* Mr. Grasshopper anything?" Osceola Slug asked. "Did you think he had earned anything?"

"No, I didn't think we *owed* him anything," Abigail said, "but seeing him in tatters, so cold and hungry, I did feel sorry for him. I wanted to help. We've known the family for years. We have enjoyed their company. We thought they enjoyed ours. This is all so sad."

"If Jimmy or any of the Grasshoppers had asked for a contract to sing while you worked, do you think you would have offered that? A contract to sing?"

"Oh, no. Neither I nor any of my family would have done that. We liked having the Grasshoppers around, but we don't have enough to pay for that sort of foolishness."

"No further questions, Your Honor. The defense rests."

The closing arguments were presented the next morning. Henry Jr. spoke of the implicit worth of art. Osceola Slug discussed the value of hard work. The judge gave the charge to the jury: "The law is not only the letter but the spirit. You must ask yourselves how to balance the tangible with the intangible. What should civilized lives expect of each other? I leave judgment to you."

The jury retired to the jury room.

After a day and a half, they had reached a verdict.

The bailiff turned to Evelyn Yellow-Finch, who had been chosen as forewoman. He took the piece of paper from her and carried it to Judge Owl. Judge Owl read the paper and returned it to the bailiff, who returned it to Mrs. Yellow-Finch. "Will the plaintiff and defendants please stand?" Judge Owl asked.

The judge turned to the jury.

"You have made your decision?" he asked.

"We have, Your Honor."

"What is your finding?"

"We find for the plaintiff, granting James Ignatius Grasshopper respect and one-half of the bounty of last summer's harvest."

Immediately there was a stir in the courtroom.

Jimmy Grasshopper had tears running down his face. He
hugged his attorneys. He felt as if he could walk on air.

Jimmy grabbed his fiddle. The Ants hung their heads in shame. They had believed they would prevail, but now they would be compelled to change. Jimmy struck up a happy tune. "Come on," he urged them. "Sing with us.

Nestor took Abigail's hand and smiled at her,
and then they, too, joined the festivities.

This was a good day.